This Little Tiger book

belongs to:

_____

_____

_____

To Tim – J C

LITTLE TIGER PRESS
1 The Coda Centre, 189 Munster Road, London SW6 6AW
www.littletigerpress.com
First published in Great Britain 2012
This edition published 2013
Text and illustrations copyright © Jane Chapman 2012
Jane Chapman has asserted her right to be identified as
the author and illustrator of this work under the Copyright,
Designs and Patents Act, 1988 • A CIP catalogue record for this
book is available from the British Library • All rights reserved
ISBN 978-1-84895-305-5
LTP/1400/0528/1112
Printed in China
2 4 6 8 10 9 7 5 3 1

Jane Chapman's Down by the River

Very Special Friends

LITTLE TIGER PRESS
London

One morning, Mouse hopped to the
edge of the river. And there she sat,
waiting for her Special Friends.

Dragonflies zipped over the rushes.
Tadpoles plipped in the shallows.
Water splashed softly against
the rocks.

"Hello," said Rabbit.
"What are you doing?"
"I'm waiting for my Special
Friends," said Mouse.

"Then I will wait with you,"
said Rabbit. "May I?"

Butterflies fluttered on the breeze.
Bees buzzed in the daisies.
Ants scuttled busily in the grass.

"Oh, it's you!" laughed Frog.
"What are you doing?"

"We're waiting for Mouse's
Special Friends," said Rabbit.
"Just the weather for waiting,"
smiled Frog. "Can I join you?"

Sunshine speckled the trees.
Caterpillars munched lazily in the leaves.
A single cloud drifted in the blue, blue sky.

"Lovely day!" sang Turtle.
"Going in for a swim, Frog?"
  "Not today," said Frog.
"We're waiting…"
  "For Mouse's Special
Friends," added Rabbit.
  "Ah," said Turtle.

It was peaceful and quiet on the riverbank. Turtle shared his lunch, and when everyone was full, the ducklings cleared up the crumbs.

"Mmmmmm, delicious," sighed Rabbit.
"Perfect," whispered Frog.
"You picked a lovely spot for waiting,
you know, Mouse," said Turtle.
"I did," said Mouse.

Shadows edged toward the water.
Fireflies glittered like stars.
   Mouse stretched her arms out wide,
and stood up.
   "Well, I must be off," she said.

"Oh, don't give up now!" cried Rabbit.
"I'm sure they'll be here soon," said Frog.
"Just give it a bit longer," nodded Turtle.
"After all, we can wait with you."

"Wait for what?" asked Mouse.
"Your Special Friends of
course!" said Rabbit.

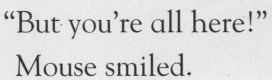

"But you're all here!"
Mouse smiled.

"Rabbit…"

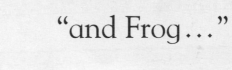

"and Frog…"

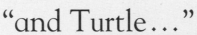

"and Turtle…"

"Who could be more
special than you?"
A rosy glow spread
over three faces.

"It has been a Special Day," said Rabbit.
"Let's wait again tomorrow!" laughed Frog.
"With apple cake," added Turtle.
"See you tomorrow then," said Mouse.
And with a happy wave she hopped
off home.

More very special stories from Little Tiger Press!

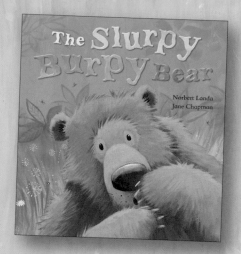

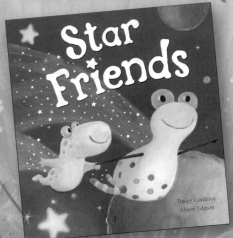

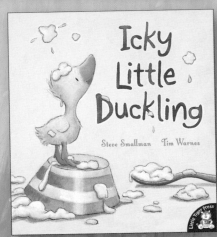

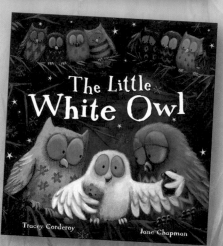

For information regarding any of the above titles or for our catalogue, please contact us:
Little Tiger Press, 1 The Coda Centre, 189 Munster Road, London SW6 6AW
Tel: 020 7385 6333 • Fax: 020 7385 7333
E-mail: info@littletiger.co.uk • www.littletigerpress.com